Praise for th...

"As grandparents of fifty gran... the *Believe and You're There* se... gather your children around you and discover the scriptures again as they come alive in the *Believe and You're There* series."

—STEPHEN AND SANDRA COVEY
Stephen Covey is the bestselling author of *7 Habits of Highly Effective People*

"Bravo! This series is a treasure! You pray that your children will fall in love with and get lost in the scriptures just as they are discovering the wonder of reading. This series does it. Two thumbs way, way up!"

—MACK AND REBECCA WILBERG
Mack Wilberg is the music director of the Mormon Tabernacle Choir

"This series is a powerful tool for helping children learn to liken the scriptures to themselves. Helping children experience the scriptural stories from their point of view is genius."

—ED AND PATRICIA PINEGAR
Ed Pinegar is the bestselling author of *Raising the Bar*

"We only wish these wonderful books had been available when we were raising our own children. How we look forward to sharing them with all our grandchildren!"

—STEPHEN AND JANET ROBINSON
Stephen Robinson is the bestselling author of *Believing Christ*

"The *Believe and You're There* series taps into the popular genre of fantasy and imagination in a wonderful way. Today's children will be drawn into the reality of events described in the scriptures. Ever true to the scriptural accounts, the authors have crafted delightful stories that will surely awaken children's vivid imaginations while teaching truths that will often sound familiar."

—TRUMAN AND ANN MADSEN
Truman Madsen is the bestselling author of *Joseph Smith, the Prophet*

"My dad and I read *At the Miracles of Jesus* together. First I'd read a chapter, and then he would. Now we're reading the next book. He says he feels the Spirit when we read. So do I."

—CASEY J., AGE 9

"My mom likes me to read before bed. I used to hate it, but the *Believe* books make reading fun and exciting. And they make you feel good inside, too."

—KADEN T., AGE 10

"Reading the *Believe* series with my tweens and my teens has been a big spiritual boost in our home—even for me! It always leaves me peaceful and more certain about what I believe."

—GLADYS A., AGE 43

"I love how Katie, Matthew, and Peter are connected to each other and to their grandma. These stories link children to their families, their ancestors, and on to the Savior. I heartily recommend them for any child, parent, or grandparent."

—ANNE S., AGE 50
Mother of ten, grandmother of nine (and counting)

When Ammon Was
a Missionary

Books in the *Believe and You're There* series

Believe and You're There

When Ammon Was a Missionary

Book 6

ALICE W· JOHNSON & ALLISON H· WARNER

DESERET
BOOK

Salt Lake City, Utah

Library of Congress Cataloging-in-Publication Data
Johnson, Alice W.
    Believe and you're there when Ammon was a missionary / Alice W. Johnson and Allison H. Warner ; illustrated by Jerry Harston and Casey Nelson.
        p. cm.
    Summary: After stepping through Grandma's new painting, Katie, Matthew, and Peter find themselves near the fields of King Lamoni, the Lamanite ruler. The children learn that loving service is the best form of missionary work.
    ISBN 978-1-60641-247-3 (paperbound)
    1. Ammon (Book of Mormon figure)—Juvenile fiction.   2. Book of Mormon stories.   3. Children's stories, American.   I. Warner, Allison H. II. Harston, Jerry, ill.   III. Nelson, Casey (Casey Shane), 1973– ill.   IV. Title.
    BX8627.4.A6J64 2010
    289.3'22—dc22   2009042216
Printed in the United States of America
R. R. Donnelley and Sons, Crawfordsville, IN

10   9   8   7   6   5   4   3   2   1

Believe in the wonder,
Believe if you dare,
Believe in your heart,
Just believe . . . and you're there!

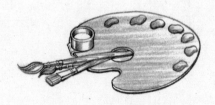

Contents

Chapter One

Starry, Starry Night

"That's easy for you to say," Katie replied to her taunting brothers, as she, Matthew, and Peter lay in sleeping bags in Grandma's backyard. The stars gleamed in the late summer night sky overhead. "You try it with one of your friends first, and let me know how it goes!"

Matthew cleared his throat and gulped at his sister's retort, his eyes sweeping the immense panorama above him. "Well, hmmm . . ."

"That's what I thought!" Katie said, feeling victorious. "It's not so easy when the shoe is on the other foot, is it, Matthew?" She spotted the North Star twinkling extra brightly above them, anchoring the Big Dipper and pointing to the Little Dipper.

"I guess not," he had to admit. "But there has to be a way. After all, missionaries do it all the time."

"That's different! They talk to people they don't even know. Aubrey is my friend, and that's the way I want it to stay," Katie explained. Aubrey and Katie had become good friends when Aubrey's family moved in across the street. Now, they both were going to start junior high next week, and they couldn't wait.

"Well, if she is really a friend, why don't you want to tell her about the gospel?" Matthew asked Katie.

"I want to tell her, but . . ." Katie hesitated.

"But what?" he asked.

"Sometimes it changes everything. Like, what if she doesn't want to hear?" Katie answered him.

Matthew nodded his head slowly. He had to admit she had a point. But how was anyone going to know how wonderful the gospel was if everyone kept it a secret?

"Okay," he said, empathizing with Katie, "I see what you're saying." But standing his ground, he added, "But there has to be a way!"

"Hey, look right up there!" Peter interjected, pointing excitedly at the night sky. "That's Pegasus! He carried lightning bolts for Zeus." Clearly, Peter had been learning about Greek myths and how constellations were named after the ancient imaginary characters in them.

Katie and Matthew looked up into the sky as Peter pointed out the stars that made up the constellation called Pegasus. As they tried to pick out the shape of a horse made by the stars, Peter announced confidently, "I wouldn't have any trouble telling one of my friends about the gospel."

Katie laughed. "I'll bet you wouldn't, little brother." Peter was fearless about talking to people. It was one of his best qualities. Right now, Katie wished she had a little more of his bravado.

"You're right, Matthew," she said, picking up their conversation again. "There just has to be a way to share the gospel without making Aubrey uncomfortable. But what is it?" Katie spoke as if she were thinking out loud.

"Look over there to the left," Peter pointed again. "That's Scorpius, the scorpion. He killed the great hunter, Orion. Only you can't see Orion in the sky until wintertime."

"How do you know so much about the stars anyway?" Matthew asked, clearly impressed.

"Don't you remember learning about those things when you were a Cub Scout?" Peter asked, scanning the sky for more constellations. "You know, Katie, if it were me, I'd just ask my friend right out, 'What do you know about The Church of Jesus Christ of Latter-day Saints?' Then I'd say, 'Do you want to learn more about it because I'd love to tell you!'"

Matthew smiled to himself. "You are quite a guy, Peter. You're a little crazy, but you get right to the point. I wish I could be more like that. I think I'd have to take it slow. I'd want to get to know the person first, and what he thinks about God and serious stuff like that. And then I would decide how to approach him."

"I've thought that maybe I could invite Aubrey to come to a church activity with me. Maybe she'd like it and would want to know more about the gospel on her own," Katie said hopefully.

"See that band of light that looks like a misty cloud? That's the Milky Way," Peter said, continuing his astronomy lesson. "That's our galaxy," he added, pointing toward the expanse of light arching in the heavens over them.

"Peter, I don't think you are listening to a word I'm saying," Katie challenged her brother.

"Why do you say that?" he asked, surprised at his sister's frustrated tone.

"Well, here I am trying to figure out what to do, and all you can talk about is the Milky Way and constellations and things like that," she countered.

"I guess you're right," Peter conceded, "but how can I lie here with all of those stars up there and not think about how amazing they are?"

"Yeah, but what about me and my problem?" Katie pushed out her bottom lip and uncharacteristically started a very convincing pout.

"Oh, come on, Sis! While I've been looking at the stars, I've been listening to everything you've said, and I've been thinking," Peter reassured her.

"So have you come up with any good ideas?" Matthew asked, curious to hear Peter's response.

"Maybe . . . well, here's what I've come up with. The Milky Way is made up of all kinds of stars, right? Some of them are really old, and some of them are young. Some shine brighter than others, some are close and some are far . . ."

"Okay, okay, we get the picture. What are you getting at?" Katie interrupted, sounding a little antsy.

"Here's my point," Peter responded. "Stars are kind of like people. All of us are different from each other, too—just like stars. And since there are lots of different kinds of people, there must be lots of different ways to tell them about the gospel. My way is to just tell people straight out. And Matthew wants to get to know people first and think about the best way to approach them. It seems to me that your way, Sis, might be to first be a good friend to the person—just like you already are—and then show her what the gospel is all about just by how you live it. Remember how you made chocolate-chip cookies to welcome Aubrey to the neighborhood? And then you helped Aubrey and her mom organize their garage after they were moved in. It seems like you're a good example of a Latter-day Saint for Aubrey already."

Katie's eyes widened in wonder with every word her little brother uttered. "Peter, I am inspired by what you're saying! You really have been thinking, haven't you?"

"I guess so." Peter smiled bashfully.

"I'll just have to summon up my courage and figure out a way to talk to Aubrey," Katie mumbled as she closed her heavy eyelids.

"Speaking of courage, do you know who had a lot of courage?" Peter asked, and then answered his own question. "It was Hercules. See his constellation right over there? He was sent on twelve labors for

Zeus. On the first one, he killed the Nemean lion. Then, let's see . . . what was his second big task?"

That was the last thing Katie and Matthew heard. Sleep overcame them, and they nodded off peacefully beneath the magical stars of the Milky Way.

Chapter Two

More Than Coincidence

The next morning as Katie gazed up at the craggy crests cutting into the emerging morning sky, she remembered Aubrey, recently moved from Texas, saying that she felt the tall peaks surrounding their small, protected valley were going to fall down on her. Katie was chuckling silently at the memory when the familiar slap of Grandma's screen door jolted her back to the present. "Good morning, everyone!" Grandma greeted them cheerily.

"It's too bad the boys aren't awake yet," she said loudly to Katie, as she surveyed the two motionless sleeping bags on the lawn. "I suppose you and I will simply have to eat the hot waffles by ourselves."

Without missing a beat, Matthew and Peter jumped up and raced each other to the kitchen.

A short time later, Matthew munched happily on a strip of savory bacon as he asked, "Grandma, is your new painting ready?"

"Well! What with the waffles and all, I thought you'd forgotten about my new painting," Grandma teased.

"Are you kidding?" Peter asked, his mouth dropping open. "How could we forget that?"

"Well, you happen to be in luck, kids. There's a brand new painting sitting on the easel in the art cottage right now!" Grandma beamed as she delivered the good news.

"Right now? Let's go!" Peter chugged down the last of his orange juice and headed for the door.

"Not so fast," Grandma stopped him with a smile. "Katie and I have to finish our waffles first. But if you're really in a hurry, you could start the dishes," Grandma suggested, thoroughly amused.

Katie and Grandma cleverly timed their breakfast to be finished just as the dishes were completed. As they put the last forkfuls of food in their mouths, they were whisked out the back door by two very eager boys.

Hurrying along the flagstone path, Peter and Matthew danced excitedly, circling around Grandma and Katie, chanting, "Believe, believe, believe! Believe, believe, believe!"

They arrived at the cottage door, the boys breathless and Katie and Grandma laughing. "All that's left is for me to open this door," Grandma said, as she reached in her pocket, produced the key, and unlocked the door to the magical world of the art cottage. "Let's hear that password, kids. That is, if you have enough breath left to get it out."

Still jostling and laughing, the children chanted in unison the mysterious poem Grandma had inscribed in the front of their journals:

"Believe in the wonder,

Believe if you dare,

Believe in your hearts,"

And then, after taking a big breath, they all shouted with gleeful, giggling abandon,

"Just believe . . . and you're there!"

Still laughing, the children flopped down on the pillows in front of the easel, and Grandma sank thankfully into her rocking chair.

"You were certainly up late last night, children," Grandma said, as she settled herself. "You must have been discussing something very interesting."

"Oh, we were," Peter spoke enthusiastically. "I

was telling Matthew and Katie all about the constellations and how they got their names." Then his voice dropped a bit, and he sounded thoughtful and earnest. "And we were working on a problem. Katie has this new friend, Aubrey, who just moved in across our street. We were trying to help Katie get up the courage to tell Aubrey about the gospel."

"You might say we were figuring out how to be missionaries," Matthew explained.

"I'd say that's quite a coincidence, when you consider my new painting and the story we're going to read today. But then, I've always believed that some things are more than coincidence," Grandma mused, with a knowing smile on her face. "When you talk about missionaries, you surely have to think of Ammon, a great missionary from the Book of Mormon."

"Yeah!" Peter declared, his eyes lighting up. "He's the one who cut off the arms!"

Katie grimaced. "Why do you have to bring up that part?"

"Let's get the story straight from the beginning, shall we, kids?" Grandma picked up her Book of Mormon and began turning its pages.

"Aren't you going to show us the painting?" Peter asked, the suspense nearly killing him.

"All in good time, my boy." Grandma smiled down at her impatient grandson. "Let's see . . . here we are. Ammon was one of the four sons of good King Mosiah. But in his youth, he was not so good himself. Ammon and his brothers and their friend, Alma the Younger, went about trying to destroy the Church and threatening the believers."

"I know! And an angel appeared to them, and his voice sounded like thunder, and it shook the ground, and they fell down to the ground like they were dead," Matthew said excitedly.

"Yes, that's right," Grandma said. "And then . . . " she went on.

"Oh no, you're not going to tell the whole thing, are you? We'll be here for days!" Peter said with dismay.

Grandma laughed. "Why don't I give you a very short version that will set the stage for the painting, and then we'll uncover it. Will that work, my impatient Peter?"

"Okay, okay," Peter agreed.

"Here goes, then." Grandma talked briskly. "After the angel came, Alma, Ammon, and his brothers realized how bad they had been. They repented of all they had done and tried to make things better for the Church and its members. Now their father, Mosiah, was the king, and he was getting old. He was going to turn over the kingdom to his sons. Ammon would have been the new king. But instead of accepting their father's offer, they decided to be missionaries instead. They loved the gospel now, and they wanted to bring souls to Christ. They went to different places to preach the word of God. And Ammon," Grandma took a deep breath, "went to the land of Ishmael. Did everyone follow that?" The children nodded emphatically.

"All right, Peter," Grandma addressed the anxious boy. "The moment has come! Why don't you uncover the painting, and we'll get to our story?"

Peter sprang to his feet and whisked the sheet off the painting. The scene Grandma had painted was of a green, grassy pasture, dotted with dozens of grazing sheep, tended by several shepherds. Behind the pasture was a large, primitive-looking city with adobe homes built into the terraced hills. Perched right in the city's center was a sprawling, grand building shaped like a pyramid. A pathway cut along the

hillside from the huge building to the low, lush pastureland.

Peter flashed an impish smile at his brother and sister and flopped back on his pillow. "Go ahead, Grandma, we're all ears," he said, confident that a new adventure was about to unfold.

"I know this is not usual, but today I would like to start with a song I learned from my grandmother." Grandma began to sing in her sweet wobbly voice:

I can share the gospel while still in tender youth,
Telling others all about its plain and precious truth.
But sometimes I am worried they might not want to hear
About the restoration of the church I hold so dear.
Service and friendship and courage in my heart
Are just the missionary tools to help me do my part.
For if I help but one soul hold fast the iron rod,
How great shall be the joy I feel when I return to God.

As Grandma finished, Katie couldn't help thinking that the story of Ammon just might hold the answer to her Aubrey problem.

Chapter Three

"We Come in Peace"

Grandma picked up her Book of Mormon, adjusted her reading glasses, and began reading aloud. "'And as Ammon entered the land of Ishmael, the Lamanites took him and bound him, as was their custom to bind all the Nephites who fell into their hands, and carry them before the king.'"

Katie, Matthew, and Peter sat poised on their pillows, prepared to leave the art cottage at the slightest movement in the painting.

Grandma read on. "'And thus Ammon was carried before the king who was over the land of Ishmael; and his name was Lamoni; and he was a descendant of Ishmael.'"

"Eeee!" A little squeaking sound escaped Katie's lips as she caught sight of one of the king's shepherds strolling slowly with the sheep along the path that led from the king's stables to the pastures.

A grin spread across Peter's excited face, and he rubbed his hands together in anticipation of the children's impending departure.

"'And after [Ammon] had been in the service of the king three days, as he was with the Lamanitish servants going forth . . .'" Grandma continued reading, but not one of her three grandchildren heard a word she read.

Keeping their eyes glued to the canvas on the easel, they silently linked hands. Peter thrust his hand into the painting, and . . . WHOOSH! The air swirled forcefully around the children, lifting them easily from their soft pillows in the art cottage, carrying them through the air for a short moment, and depositing them safely in the land of Ishmael. The journey seemed to take but an instant.

"That was quick!" Peter declared, gasping for breath as the dusty air settled around them.

"I'll say!" Matthew agreed. "What a ride!"

"I didn't even have time to take a breath!" Katie exhaled loudly and slowly as she turned around to inspect their surroundings. They had landed in a small clearing, sheltered by thick green bushes and tall trees. Overhead, a beautiful sky made a blue back-drop for the rich, green vegetation. Shining through the leaves, radiant beams of sunlight created intricate shadow patterns on the ground beneath them.

A well-worn dirt path cut right through the middle of the grassy clearing. One end of the clearing opened to reveal dozens of white sheep in the green pasture beyond, which sloped down to a wide, slow river. Through the trees at the other end of the clearing, the city was visible, with its low dwellings and the imposing building.

"Look how big that building is!" Peter marveled, awestruck at the sheer size of the structure.

"I'm pretty sure that is Lamoni's palace," Matthew reasoned sensibly.

"I'd have to agree, and those must be his flocks over there," Katie concluded.

As they stood inspecting the view, they heard the snap of twigs and the crackle of leaves. They realized too late that someone was running toward the clearing where they stood. A panicked look crossed Katie's face, and she stood frozen, her eyes searching for a place to hide. But there was no time. A brown-skinned, dark-haired boy about Matthew's age burst into the clearing before any of them could move a muscle.

"Oh, no," Matthew muttered under his breath, "now what?"

He didn't have to wait long to find out. The boy, who was as startled as the three children, let out a loud whoop. Then, turning on them, he expertly twirled the staff he carried in his hand, bringing it to rest on Matthew's chest and demanding, "Who are you?"

Matthew opened his mouth, but couldn't speak. He looked to Katie, and, from the look on her face, Matthew feared she was going to cry—or faint. He fumbled for her hand, ready to escape at a moment's notice. He could feel that she was shaking all over.

All of a sudden, before Matthew could grab his hand, Peter piped up cheerily, "Hey, that was cool. Do you know any more karate?"

Moving his staff to Peter's chest, the boy's eyes narrowed, and he repeated his demand, this time

more forcefully, "Who are you, and what are you doing here?"

Suddenly Matthew noticed that, although the Lamanite boy's words sounded brave, the staff he held to Peter's chest was quivering. Perhaps, Matthew thought, the boy was as frightened as they were.

Peter responded, "I'm Peter." And then, imitating his favorite animated movie character, he added emphatically, "We come in peace."

"You come in peace?" the boy asked hopefully.

Finding his voice, Matthew jumped in. "Yes, we do. We come in peace."

The Lamanite boy lowered his staff slowly, obviously more relaxed, but still a little cautious. He asked again, this time more kindly, "And why are you here?"

"We wanted to see the king's sheep and visit your beautiful city," Matthew answered simply, gesturing first to the pastures and then to the nearby town.

"Are you Nephites?" the boy asked.

"No, we're Americans. We come from up north of here," Peter said proudly.

"I am very relieved," the boy said thankfully. "When I saw your light hair, I was afraid you were Nephites, coming to do us harm. I've never heard of

Americans, but as long as you are not Nephites . . . and you do seem nice . . . I am sorry if I scared you with my staff." He looked meaningfully at Katie as he apologized.

"Oh, don't worry," she laughed, "I'm just fine." Katie's voice sounded high and nervous, and she was not entirely convincing.

"Forgive me, please. My name is Gid. I am the son of Mishgar."

"I'm Katie, and these are my brothers, Matthew and Peter." Then she added haltingly, "We are the children of Walter."

Gid seemed to accept this readily, and he smiled in forthright friendship as he said, "I am on my way to fetch something for my father. He is in the pastures down by the river with the king's sheep. Would you like to come with me?"

"Yes, of course we would." Peter accepted the invitation immediately.

"We do have one problem." Gid furrowed his brow and ran his finger through his dark hair.

"What's that?" Matthew asked.

"Well, we are Lamanites here. You can tell by our dark skin and hair. Your skin is much too light. People might think you are Nephites, like I did.

Then they would bind you and take you to prison," Gid explained, clearly concerned.

"I see the problem," Matthew said, holding his fair-skinned arm next to Gid's brown one.

"I have an idea," Peter said, scooping up some of the rich, dark dirt covering the ground. It was so heavy and moist, it felt almost like clay. "Let's rub some of this dirt on our skin." He covered his face and arms with the reddish-brown loam and then started on his legs. When he finished, he looked to Gid for his approval.

Gid inspected him from top to bottom and nodded. "Yes," he said. "I think that will work very nicely."

Katie and Matthew scooped up big handfuls of dirt and transformed themselves into Lamanites, too. "Hmm," Gid said as he walked around them, inspecting them carefully. "Just one more thing," he said, taking the wide sash from his waist. "Katie, your hair is the most unusual color I have ever seen. It's the color of gold. We must cover it." Gid placed the sash on Katie's head, spreading it carefully to cover her hair, and then tied it on top in a large, firm knot.

When he was finished, he took one more long,

careful look at the three of them. Satisfied at last, he nodded and announced, "Come, my Lamanite friends. Let us be off!"

Chapter Four

A Friend to the King

The four children began walking toward the city in high spirits. Gid was proud of his flourishing hometown, and he was looking forward to pointing out the interesting sights to his new friends.

Katie and Peter walked in front of Matthew and Gid, who had quickly struck up a ready friendship.

"My father works for the king," Gid informed all his visitors. "He is the chief of all the keepers of the king's flocks."

"I knew a shepherd once," Peter exclaimed. "He lived near Bethlehem."

"That must be far away from here. I have never heard of it," Gid responded.

"Oh, yes. It is very far away," Matthew jumped right in, preventing Peter from saying more. "It is so far away that we have only been there once."

Katie joined the rescue, quickly changing the subject. "Does your father like being a shepherd?" she inquired of Gid.

"Yes, but it can be dangerous. When he takes the sheep to drink at the waters of Sebus, sometimes robbers come and scatter the flocks. Then, before the sheep can be gathered, the robbers sneak away with a few."

"Why is that so dangerous for the shepherds? Do the robbers try to hurt them?" Katie asked.

"No, that is not the problem. The king gets very angry with the shepherds when the sheep they are watching get scattered and stolen. He has even ordered that some shepherds be killed as punishment," Gid explained solemnly.

"Gid! Gid! There you are!" someone yelled frantically, approaching the children from behind.

They all turned to see a man running toward them as fast as he could go.

"Father!" Gid answered, his voice filled with concern. "What is it? What has happened?"

The panting man paused, doubled over with his hands on his knees, breathless from running. Between gasps, he wheezed, "The sheep . . . waters of Sebus . . . Ammon . . . arms. Can't stop now . . . ," he continued, motioning for them to follow. "Must tell the king . . . come!"

"Come on!" Gid dashed off to catch up with his father. "Follow me," he called to the three bewildered children.

Peter took off, keeping Gid in his sights. Matthew grabbed Katie by the hand and followed behind, running to keep up.

"Matthew, are we going where I think we're going?" Katie managed to ask.

"You mean the palace?" Matthew asked, not slowing down.

"Uh-huh," Katie half-moaned her response.

"That's what I'm thinking," he replied.

"Oh, no!" This time she wailed loudly, stopping

in her tracks. "Don't tell me we are going to have to see all those arms!"

"We can't worry about that now, Sis! We're going to lose the others if we don't hurry up." Matthew grabbed Katie's hand and sprinted around a corner, which opened up into a small marketplace. Matthew spied Peter and Gid just as they disappeared through a large, stone archway on the other side of the market.

"Come on, Sis, we're almost there," Matthew encouraged Katie, as he dragged her through the marketplace, darting in and out of the stands and people.

As they passed through the arch, they found themselves in a grand plaza, right in the center of the city. At the far end of the plaza, the mammoth palace towered above them. It was a sprawling, pyramid-shaped structure, made up of many smaller buildings on different levels. The walls were decorated with rich, colorful paintings and elaborate carvings. Stone stairs led up the center of the structure, interrupted by a smaller plaza halfway to the top. The stairs continued from the small plaza to the uppermost part of the palace. This highest level was flat, protected from the blazing sun by a large canopy held aloft by four ornate, wooden posts.

"There they are!" Katie called out, spotting the others at the base of the palace stairs.

They caught up to Mishgar and the boys. Mishgar and his fellow servants were gathered there, talking excitedly. Several of the servants carried bulky bundles covered with large pieces of leather.

"There you are!" Peter cried, giving Matthew a big bear hug. "We lost you in the crowd."

"We were right behind you," Matthew said, "but someone slowed me down a bit." He gestured with his head toward his big sister, rolling his eyes just a bit.

"What are those men carrying?" Katie asked nervously.

Peter grimaced. "Those are the arms that Ammon chopped off of the Lamanite robbers."

"You just stay right over here." Matthew put himself between Katie and the men with the arms.

Mishgar hurried back to the children. "Come, Gid. We shepherds are going into King Lamoni's court to tell him of Ammon's bravery. You can come, if you like."

"These are my new friends, Father. They are called Matthew, Katie, and Peter," Gid said, gesturing to each child in turn. "May they come in too?"

31

"Sure, sure," said Mishgar, distracted by the thought of telling the king what had happened. "You and your friends stand at the back of the court and be very quiet," Mishgar instructed. Solemnly and silently, the four children nodded their understanding.

The servants led the way into the palace and its throne room, and each in turn laid his bundle in front of the king's throne.

From the back of the large chamber, the children stood quietly, awestruck by the commanding presence of the king and his many attendants. The king sat at the front of the huge chamber on his raised, rich-looking throne, flanked on either side by servants and advisors.

But it was the king himself, clothed in exotic, royal attire, at whom the children couldn't stop staring. A jaguar-skin skirt hung from his waist, held in place by a belt made of shiny silver chains adorned with the long, pointy teeth of wild animals. A netted jade collar was fastened around his neck, and a colorful headdress with plumes of blue and green quetzal feathers sat upon his head. Mishgar and the other servants knelt at his feet.

"Stand forth and testify concerning this matter," King Lamoni commanded the servants.

As chief shepherd, Mishgar spoke first. Then each shepherd, in turn, told of the things which he had seen at the waters of Sebus. It seemed that a group of thieves, whooping and charging wildly, had come to frighten and scatter the sheep. But the newest shepherd, Ammon, just three days on the job, calmly told the other shepherds to gather the flocks. Then he faced the marauding enemy alone.

First, he killed six men using his sling. Then the robbers, angry with Ammon for slaying their brethren, went after him with their swords. Mishgar described what happened next. "Every time a man lifted his club to smite Ammon, Ammon smote off his arms with his sword. He withstood the enemies' blows by smiting their arms with the edge of his sword, and he caused them to flee by the strength of his arm."

The king was astonished and said, "Surely, this is more than a man. Behold, is not this the Great Spirit who doth send such great punishments upon this people, because of their murders?"

Mishgar answered, "Whether he be the Great Spirit or a man, we know not. . . . We know that he is a friend to the king. And now, O king, we do not believe that a man has such great power, for we know he cannot be slain."

When King Lamoni heard these words, he said, "Now I know that it is the Great Spirit; and he has come down at this time to preserve your lives, that I might not slay you as I did your brethren."

"What does he mean by 'the Great Spirit'?" Peter asked Gid in a low whisper.

"To us, the Great Spirit is God. I think the king is afraid that he has done wrong in the past to kill his servants when sheep were lost or stolen. And he fears that the Great Spirit has come down to stop him from doing it again," Gid replied.

"I guess his conscience is getting the better of him," Katie commented.

Everyone was quiet, waiting for the king to go on. The king shifted from one side to the other in his seat. Finally he asked, "Where is this man that has such great power?"

"As you commanded earlier in the day, he is feeding your horses and preparing your chariots to take you to tonight's feast at your father's house," Mishgar replied.

The king was amazed by this news. First,

Ammon had risked his own life to save the sheep—and he had defeated the robbers all by himself. And now, instead of expecting a hero's welcome, he was out in the stables tending to the horses!

The astonished king said to all in his court, "Surely there has not been any servant among all my servants that has been so faithful as this man; for even he doth remember all my commandments to execute them. Now I surely know that this is the Great Spirit, and I would desire him that he come in unto me, but I durst not." He sank back in his seat and closed his eyes, deep in thought.

"I think the king really wants to ask Ammon to come to him, but he's worried about what Ammon will think of him," Katie murmured softly in Matthew's ear.

"Isn't that how we all are sometimes? We want to be close to Heavenly Father, but we're afraid to ask Him to be near because we're not perfect yet," Matthew answered Katie with the very kind of insight she had come to expect from her thoughtful brother.

"It's funny," she replied to Matthew. "Even though Lamoni is a king, he's a lot like the rest of us, isn't he?"

Chapter Five

"I Am a Man"

As he had been instructed earlier that morning, Ammon now worked steadily in the stables to prepare the horses and chariots for King Lamoni's upcoming journey. While the king's court was marveling at Ammon's miraculous feats, Ammon worked away until he was satisfied that everything was in order. Only then did he prepare himself to be presented in the king's court.

Ammon climbed the stairs to the palace and strode with calm assurance across the central courtyard toward the royal chamber. He paused before entering. The noble men and women of the court were outfitted in extravagant plumed headdresses, luxurious animal skins, and beaded shawls. All their finery seemed a stark contrast to Ammon's humble shepherd's clothing. But Ammon knew the Lord was with him. With quiet dignity, he approached the throne.

The king was still deeply troubled by the way he had treated his servants in the past. Furthermore, the possibility that Ammon was indeed the Great Spirit worried him greatly. His heart was heavy, and his very appearance seemed changed from the last time Ammon had been in his presence.

Ammon interpreted the change as displeasure, and he turned to leave Lamoni's presence. Lamoni motioned to one of his servants, who called after Ammon, "Rabbanah."

Peter nudged Gid and whispered, "What does 'rabbanah' mean?"

Gid whispered back, "It means 'great and powerful king.'"

"Oh." Peter nodded his understanding, although he thought it was interesting that a humble shepherd was called "great king" right in front of Lamoni, perched on a grand throne in a magnificent palace.

"Rabbanah," the servant continued, "the king desireth thee to stay."

Ammon stopped and turned, squared his shoulders, and stepped forward to face the king.

Respectfully, he asked, "What wilt thou that I should do for thee, O king?"

Lamoni sat in total silence for an hour—a whole hour! He seemed too troubled to speak. No one in the throne room dared move. Even Peter was unusually still. Ammon waited patiently for the king's answer. Sensing that a mighty struggle was taking place in the king's heart, Ammon prompted him again, asking, "What desirest thou of me?"

Still, Lamoni gave no answer.

Filled with the Spirit, Ammon perceived the thoughts of the king. He stepped forward and addressed the silent king once more. "Is it because thou hast heard that I defended thy servants and thy flocks, and slew seven of their brethren with the sling and with the sword, and smote off the arms of others, in order to defend thy flocks and thy servants; behold, is it this that causeth thy marvelings?"

And then Ammon answered the king's most burning question with this simple, clear statement: "Behold, I am a man, and am thy servant; therefore, whatsoever thou desirest which is right, that will I do."

In wonder and surprise, the king opened his

mouth and asked Ammon, "Who art thou? Art thou that Great Spirit, who knows all things?"

Ammon said simply, "I am not."

Still unable to grasp how Ammon could know what he was thinking, the astonished king questioned him again. "How knowest thou the thoughts of my heart? Thou mayest speak boldly, and tell me concerning these things; and also tell me by what power ye slew and smote off the arms of my brethren that scattered my flocks—and now, if thou wilt tell me concerning these things, whatsoever thou desirest I will give unto thee."

Filled with the spirit of missionary work, Ammon replied, "Wilt thou hearken unto my words, if I tell thee by what power I do these things? And this is the thing that I desire of thee."

The king answered, "Yea, I will believe all thy words."

Ammon continued with boldness, "Believest thou that there is a God?"

The king looked puzzled and answered, "I do not know what that meaneth."

"Believest thou that there is a Great Spirit?" Ammon asked.

"Yea," the king said.

"This is God," Ammon explained, and then asked, "Believest thou that this Great Spirit, who is God, created all things which are in heaven and in the earth?"

Lamoni nodded. "Yea, I believe that he created all things which are in the earth." Then he admitted, "But I do not know the heavens."

"The heavens," Ammon went on, "is a place where God dwells and all his holy angels."

"Is it above the earth?" asked Lamoni.

"Yea, and he looketh down upon all the children of men; and he knows all the thoughts and intents of the heart; for by his hand were they all created from the beginning."

King Lamoni said, "I believe all these things which thou hast spoken. Art thou sent from God?"

Ammon replied, "I am a man; and man in the beginning was created after the image of God, and I am called by his Holy Spirit to teach these things unto this people, that they may be brought to a knowledge of that which is just and true; and a portion of that Spirit dwelleth in me, which giveth me knowledge, and also power according to my faith and desires which are in God."

Then Ammon taught King Lamoni and his

servants. He began at the creation of the world. He taught them all that the prophets had spoken, and he laid before them all that was contained in the holy scriptures. He taught them of their ancestors, Lehi and Ishmael, who had left Jerusalem, and of their journey in the wilderness. He told them of the hardships that Lehi and his family had experienced. He gave an account of the rebellion of Laman and Lemuel and the sons of Ishmael. Then he told of the records that had been kept from the time that Lehi left Jerusalem to the present time.

Ammon went on to teach them all about the plan of redemption, the plan prepared before the world began. He told them about Jesus Christ, who was soon to come to live on earth, and how He would suffer for our sins so that all repentant people could be redeemed and return to live with God in glory.

Lamoni and all in the court listened intently to what Ammon taught, and they believed his words. When Ammon finished, the king, realizing his need to be redeemed, cried out to the Lord, "O Lord, have mercy; according to thy abundant mercy which thou hast had upon the people of Nephi, have upon me, and my people." When Lamoni had uttered these words, he collapsed, falling forward onto the ground.

His terrified servants rushed forward, surrounding him. "Quickly, get some water," one shouted.

One servant removed Lamoni's headdress and laid the king's head upon his cape. "King, my king, wake up, wake up!" he called frantically, lightly striking the king's cheeks to rouse him. But all the servant's efforts were in vain. Lamoni remained still and lifeless on the floor.

Panic broke out in the chamber. Some servants cried out, "He's dead! The king is dead!"

"No! It cannot be!" others wailed.

In the back corner of the chamber, Gid, Matthew, Peter, and Katie huddled close together to escape the escalating chaos.

Gid, his heart beating fast, looked around the room for Mishgar. "Where is my father?" he asked, his voice full of concern.

"There he is," said Peter, pointing. Mishgar hovered over the king, pressing a flask of water to his lips, hoping for him to swallow some. But it was no use. Lamoni lay unmoving on the cold stone floor.

"Stand back," one of the king's servants ordered. "We must take him unto the queen."

A stunned silence filled the crowded chamber. The king, it seemed, was dead. The people of his court looked on, horrified, as Lamoni's loyal servants came forward, lifted the king's lifeless body to their shoulders, and solemnly carried it away.

Chapter Six

"He Doth Not Stink"

The moment the king's body left the royal chamber, pandemonium broke out. As the panic rose, Mishgar fought his way through the distraught courtiers to find his son, Gid, and Gid's three friends, now pressed into the back corner of the chamber.

"Come quickly," he said, taking Gid's hand. "There is such chaos here, we will be much safer if we return home and wait for news there."

Following Mishgar and Gid, the children were carried along by the crowds fleeing the palace in fear. The streets were filled with frantic, frightened people. Matthew tried to stay close to Mishgar and Gid, but amidst all the confusion, he lost sight of his Lamanite friends.

"Where have they gone?" Katie moaned desperately.

"They were just up ahead, but . . . but I can't see them just now," Matthew replied, sounding nearly as desperate.

"Oh, no," Katie wailed again. "What if we can't find them? Then what are we going to do?"

Matthew took her hand and pulled her through the crowd behind him. Maybe they could make it back to the quiet clearing where they had landed, he thought to himself.

"Wait for me!" Peter called, afraid he'd be left behind. He grabbed Katie's hand. The children were now connected, and instantly the turmoil that surrounded them became silence. Weightless, they were carried swiftly through space and time to the safety and serenity of the art cottage.

Just as they had left her, Grandma sat in her rocker, calmly reading aloud the account of Lamoni from the scriptures. Her voice was soothing and tranquil. "'And it came to pass that his servants took him and carried him in unto his wife, and laid him upon a bed.'"

Katie quickly looked over at Matthew and Peter, worried they might still be dressed in their Lamanite tunics. Thankfully, the boys were in the same T-shirts and jeans as before, but Peter's cheek was smudged with dirt.

"Peter, your cheek," she whispered and pointed, so Grandma wouldn't hear.

He grabbed the bottom of his shirt and quickly wiped the dirt off.

"Thanks," he said, smiling at Katie gratefully. But when he caught sight of his sister, his eyes got big, and he pointed wildly at her head. Katie's hands shot up, where she discovered Gid's red sash still covering her hair.

"Thanks," she mouthed

silently, as she hastily unwound the sash and tied it around her waist.

"That was close," Matthew murmured softly.

"I'll say!" Katie mouthed, letting out a big breath. She checked to see if Grandma noticed anything, but Grandma read on unfazed, engrossed in the fate of Lamoni.

"'And he lay as if he were dead for the space of two days and two nights; and his wife, and his sons, and his daughters mourned over him, after the manner of the Lamanites, greatly lamenting his loss.'"

"So, is the king really dead or not?" Peter interrupted Grandma.

"Well, everyone thinks he is, don't they?" Grandma replied.

"He looked pretty dead to me," Peter announced confidently.

"Oh, really?" Grandma looked quizzically at her grandson.

"What an imagination you have, buddy," Matthew said, laughing nervously and patting Peter on the back. "Why don't we let Grandma finish the story?"

"Okay, go on, Grandma," Peter encouraged her. "I promise I'll be quiet."

"'Good idea!" Katie said, giving him a stern look. This wasn't the first time Peter had nearly spilled the beans about their time travels.

"'And it came to pass,'" Grandma went on, "'that after two days and two nights they were about to take his body and lay it in a sepulchre . . .'"

"A what?" Peter couldn't help asking Katie.

"It's a tomb, remember?" Katie whispered. "Keep listening."

All the time Grandma was reading, the painting on the easel remained still and lifeless. There had been no sign of movement since they had returned. Surely, Katie thought, this couldn't be the end of their adventure!

"Grandma, could you fast forward a little? I can't wait to hear what happens." Impatient Peter was practically pleading.

"Well, let's see. The queen calls for Ammon and he goes to her."

"I remember this part," Matthew jumped in. "The king lay on his bed for two days, and most people thought he should be buried."

"Oh, yeah," Katie remembered, giggling. "They said that the king 'stinketh.' It says so right in the scriptures! But the queen thinks they're all wrong. She says, 'To me, he doth not stink.'"

"That was her way of saying she didn't think her husband was really dead, right, Grandma?" Matthew asked.

"Right," Grandma agreed. "She said to Ammon, 'The servants of my husband have made it known unto me that thou art a prophet of a holy God, and that thou hast power to do many mighty works in his name; therefore, if this is the case, I would that ye should go in and see my husband.'"

Then Grandma posed an important question. "Now, children, why do you think the queen wanted Ammon to go see the king?"

"Well," Matthew was the first one to answer, "I think she was hoping that Ammon could wake him up."

"That's what I think, too, Matthew. But Ammon knew that Lamoni was under the power of God. This is how the scriptures describe what was happening to Lamoni: 'The dark veil of unbelief was being cast away from his mind, and . . . the light of the glory of God . . . lit up in his soul, . . . and he was carried away in God.' Ammon knew that this is what was happening, so after he went in to see the king, he said to the queen: 'He is not dead, but he sleepeth in God, and on the morrow he shall rise again; therefore bury him not.'"

"The queen must have been so relieved!" Katie exclaimed.

"I'll say—if she believed Ammon, that is. Did she, Grandma? Did she believe him?" Peter asked.

"Good question, Peter. Let's keep reading, shall we?" Grandma replied. "'Ammon said unto her: Believest thou this? And she said unto him: I have had no witness save thy word, and the word of our servants; nevertheless I believe that it shall be according as thou hast said.

"'And Ammon said unto her: Blessed art thou because of thy exceeding faith; I say unto thee, woman, there has not been such great faith among all the people of the Nephites. And it came to pass that she watched over the bed of her husband, from that time even until that time on the morrow which Ammon had appointed that he should rise. And it came to pass that he arose, according to the words of Ammon.'"

"Wow! I guess that proved that Ammon really was a prophet of God!" Peter exulted.

"And that the queen was right to have such great faith in what he said," Katie pointed out.

Katie turned to study the painting once again. To her amazement, this time the painting was alive with tiny figures running toward the palace.

"Matthew, look," she whispered, nudging him.

"I see it, Sis," he whispered back.

As they watched, scores of people thronged the palace steps, moving about as if they were talking excitedly.

"Let's go see what's happening," she whispered, undoing the sash from around her waist and quickly tying it over her hair.

Peter noticed the moving people in the painting, too. His eager eyes came alive. "Oh boy, can we go?" he mouthed, with a glance toward Grandma, who was still engrossed in the scriptures.

Quietly, all three children arose as one. Matthew's face shone with anticipation, and he offered one hand to his brother. Peter took hold of it, and Katie took the other, as Peter thrust his free hand right into the painting. Just as had happened before, the air began swirling around them, lifting them off the ground . . . and in the blink of an eye, Grandma and the art cottage were gone. In what felt like no time at all, the children came to rest, unnoticed, on the crowded steps of Lamoni's palace. They found themselves surrounded by dozens of Lamanites, discussing with each other, in wonder, the amazing events of the day.

Chapter Seven

The Spirit of the Lord

As they stood on the steps of the palace, in the midst of the teeming multitude, the children heard talk of Lamoni's miraculous awakening rippling through the crowd. Small groups of people bunched together, marveling at what had taken place. "He lives! The king has come back!" people exclaimed in wonder.

Even as the good news spread, some in the crowd came from the royal chamber, now telling a new tale—this one not so happy. Confusion quickly rolled through the bewildered throng.

"The king has collapsed again," the cry went out, "and this time, the queen has collapsed with him."

Gasps of disbelief filled the air. "The queen?" a woman whimpered somewhere behind them. "Who will be next?"

"What of Ammon?" another cried. "Where is he?"

"He, too, has fallen to the ground, and all the king's servants with him," a loud voice in the crowd answered back.

"Come on! Let's get a better look," Peter urged Matthew and Katie, and he disappeared into the dense crowd.

"Peter!" Matthew called after him. "Wait for us!" But undaunted, Peter forged ahead.

"It's no use, Sis," Matthew said shaking his head. "Come on, we'll just have to go in there and get him."

"Another adventure, compliments of our little brother," Katie muttered, grabbing Matthew's hand as he was swallowed by the crowd.

Inside the royal chamber, the crowd was even thicker. "Excuse us, excuse us," Matthew repeated again and again, as they inched toward the throne.

Finally, they pushed through the last of the people surrounding the king. In front of them, Lamoni lay again on the cold stone floor, with the queen, his servants, and Ammon lying near him.

Nearby, Peter stood with the crowd surrounding him. He waved them over. "Hey guys, look!" he said, pointing to the scene before them. "They all look like they're dead, but they're really not!"

"Peter, Katie, Matthew." Someone was softly calling their names. "Over here!"

That could only mean one thing! Gid must be here! They spotted Gid and his father making their way toward them along the perimeter of crowd. Gid waved and flashed them an enormous smile.

Katie smiled back. "It makes me feel so much better to know they are here," she said, relief washing over her.

Mishgar and Gid slid in beside the children, greeting them with warm hand clasps and pats on the back. Then the questions flew.

"Where have you been? I haven't seen you for three days. Have you heard what has happened?" Gid asked.

"We have heard some of it, but why is everyone lying on the ground?" Peter questioned him.

"You should have been here!" Gid began. "The king miraculously awakened after three days, just as Ammon said he would. As he arose, he stretched out his hand to the queen, and declared, 'Blessed be the name of God, and blessed art thou.' Then he went on to testify with great power, 'For as sure as thou livest, behold, I have seen my Redeemer; . . . and he shall redeem all mankind who believe on his name.'"

"You should have seen his face as he spoke. It was filled with pure joy—greater joy than I have ever witnessed," Mishgar added. "The joy seemed to overwhelm him, and he sank to the ground again, just as he did before."

"He saw Jesus," Katie said reverently, awed by the thought of it.

"Just hearing that gives me goose bumps all over," Matthew shivered. "It makes me so happy!"

"Now you know how the queen must have felt, because she was overcome like Lamoni, and she fell to the floor, too," Gid went on. Then looking Matthew in the eye, he said softly, "I felt such a powerful feeling here," he gestured to his heart, "a feeling I have never felt before."

Matthew rested his hand on Gid's shoulder. "That must be the Spirit of the Lord," he explained.

"Then Ammon must have felt it, too. After the king and queen were overcome, Ammon fell to his knees and offered a prayer to God," Mishgar went on. "He thanked God for pouring out his Spirit upon the Lamanites. Then he collapsed to the ground, too."

"What about all the servants? What happened to them?" Peter asked.

"All of them began to pray to God with all their might, until one by one they were all overcome with the Spirit, and each of them fell to the ground, too," Gid went on.

"Every single one of them?" Katie asked.

"All but one. Her name is Abish. She is a servant to the queen," Mishgar explained.

"Why was she still standing?" Matthew was curious.

"Abish already knew about Ammon's God. She already believed in this Redeemer that visited the king," Gid said.

"But how did she learn about the Redeemer?" Matthew asked.

"Apparently, her father had a remarkable vision—maybe something like the king had while he was overcome for three days," Mishgar said.

"It must have been a really powerful experience if it convinced his daughter to believe, too," Katie observed.

"Yes," Mishgar agreed thoughtfully, "it must have been."

"Where is Abish now?" Matthew asked.

"She felt the power of God when Lamoni told the court what he had seen—just like I did," Mishgar explained. "She recognized the joy in Lamoni's face. She said it was the same joy she had felt when she first heard about her father's vision. So she ran from house to house to tell everyone about what had happened. She wanted everyone to come, to see and feel

what was happening here. She wanted all of us to feel the power of God and believe in Him, too."

"So that's why there are so many people coming to the palace," Matthew reasoned.

"Judging from the size of this crowd, I guess the news has spread," Gid observed.

As the chamber filled to overflowing, alarm spread among the gathering people as they saw the king and queen lying on the ground, surrounded by their servants. All the bodies lying on the stone floor appeared to be dead. Shouts of anger and fear echoed all around.

"This great evil has come upon the king and his household because he allowed a Nephite to come among us. He should have known better!" shouted a man standing near Peter.

Then, from the far side of the chamber, another man declared emphatically, "The king brought this calamity upon himself! Had he not killed the servants whose flocks were scattered at the waters of Sebus, surely this would not have happened."

Suddenly, a cry went up from a gang of unkempt, wild-looking men, rapidly making their way to where the king and the others lay upon the ground.

The crowd parted as the leader of the gang forced his way through, followed by his men.

Emboldened by the accusations he had heard, he shouted, "This man," and he pointed right at Ammon, "killed my friends at Sebus. He will not go unpunished!"

Another man in the gang rushed forward, his hand firmly gripping the sword on his belt. "You killed my brother!" he yelled at Ammon, who still lay as if dead. Then the man advanced menacingly, until he stood right over Ammon. The crowd gasped as he drew his sword with a flourish.

Terrified, Katie cowered behind Matthew, burying her face in her hands. "Oh, no," she wailed, "I can't bear to watch."

"Now I will take vengeance on you," the enraged man bellowed, swinging his sword high above his head, his arm now fully extended. He let out a spine-tingling scream and lunged toward Ammon, ready to strike. Then without warning, the scream turned to silence. The sword fell from the man's grasp, clanging noisily to the floor, and he crumpled to the floor, his body limp, still, and lifeless.

Chapter Eight

Of Testimony and Changing Hearts

Silence—stunned silence—filled the royal chamber. In the space of a mere instant, the man who wanted to kill Ammon had been struck dead by an unseen force, right at Ammon's feet. And Ammon still lay unmoving, completely undisturbed! A terrible fear came upon the multitude when they saw the fate of the man now dead on the floor.

A fellow shepherd grabbed Mishgar's arm. "Mishgar, what is the meaning of all this? Where does this great power come from?"

"I have seen only what you have seen," Mishgar replied. But the feelings in his heart were another matter altogether. How was he to make sense of the powerful witness he felt in his soul?

Whispers began to ripple through the crowd, and

a nearby woman declared, "Ammon is the Great Spirit, I know it." Others around her weren't so sure.

"He can't be the Great Spirit," a man near her argued. "But he must have been sent by the Great Spirit." And so the rumblings in the crowd started to swell, and on every side heated debates raged about Ammon and who he was.

Above the rest a bellow was heard. "He is not the Great Spirit. He is a monster!" The crowd roared their approval.

"He was sent here from the Nephites to torment us and cause all manner of mischief," another accuser hollered.

"We must send him back to where he came from. We don't want his kind here!" Another roar of approval went up.

"We have done wrong, and the Great Spirit has sent Ammon to correct us. We need to repent," one man insisted forcefully.

Several people in the crowd turned on him, and another man stepped forward, a sinister look on his face. "How can you say we are the ones that need to repent? This Nephite brought with him these calamities. He alone caused the destruction of so many of our brethren!" Now the crowd was an angry mob, roiling with rage.

"Are you getting a little worried?" Katie whispered to Matthew.

"A little, but if we stay close to Mishgar, I think we will be all right," Matthew answered, with more confidence than he felt. "It couldn't hurt to say a prayer though," he added.

"I already have," Katie assured Matthew.

The quarreling mounted with each passing moment. Katie was afraid a fight might break out, and someone would get hurt or killed.

Suddenly, a Lamanite woman broke through the perimeter of the crowd and stood next to the prostrate king. Gid leaned over to Matthew. "Look! That is Abish. She has returned."

Abish looked around at all the people making terrible accusations and threatening each other. It was too much for her to bear, and her face crumpled with sadness. She began to weep openly.

Then, kneeling next to the queen, Abish took her by the hand as if to raise her from the ground. The moment Abish touched her hand, the queen rose to her feet and cried in a loud voice, "O blessed Jesus, who has saved me from an awful hell! O blessed

God, have mercy on this people!" She clasped her hands with joy and continued speaking, now in strange words. "I can't tell what she is saying," Katie said. "Can you understand her?"

Matthew shook his head. "Not a word," he replied. From the puzzled looks on the faces of the onlookers, it was clear that they didn't understand the queen, either.

Then the queen went over to Lamoni, and as she took him by the hand, he arose. Filled with power and conviction, he began calling the people in the chamber to repentance. Stunned by the change in their king, many in the chamber listened intently, with softened hearts and willing ears.

"My people," the king said, "we are the sons and daughters of Ishmael, who came up out of Jerusalem with Father Lehi. Ours is a noble heritage."

"He looks different," Gid whispered to Matthew.

"He is different," Matthew said. "His heart has been changed. Now he believes in God, and in His Son, Jesus Christ. He has been converted to the true gospel."

"How would that make him so different?" Gid asked.

"Listen, and you'll see," Matthew assured him.

"I have learned of the scriptures, the records kept from Father Adam to Lehi, and from Lehi down to the present time," Lamoni continued. "But most important, I have learned of the Savior, and of His redeeming love, whereby we can be reunited with God. This knowledge fills my soul with joy."

Moved by the king's words, Gid turned to Mishgar in earnest. "How can we feel that joy, Father?"

"I am uncertain, son. Let us listen. Perhaps we will learn," Mishgar answered.

The king continued testifying, "All this is possible because of the Redeemer, Jesus Christ. He will come to the earth and suffer for our sins, that if we repent, we will be forgiven, and God will remember our sins no more. I know this is true, for I have seen Him. I believe on the name of Jesus Christ. And behold, He will redeem all who believe on His name."

The testimony of the king—the king who was once known for cruelty and brutality, but was now repentant and humble—touched those who listened. And many believed his words and were converted, too.

"Hey," Peter nudged Matthew, "why are some of the people leaving?"

"I guess some don't believe what Lamoni is saying," he told Peter sadly.

"How can they not feel that it is true?" Peter asked, dismayed by Matthew's conclusion.

"I don't know, buddy, but it seems like that is how it always is," Matthew explained. "Some people choose to open their hearts to the gospel, and some people refuse. Heavenly Father always lets us choose for ourselves."

"Look!" Katie exclaimed. "It's Ammon! He is standing up, too!"

Indeed he was. And Ammon, the missionary, began teaching the multitude with great power and authority. As he spoke, each of Lamoni's servants stood, too, and each bore testimony of what he had experienced.

"My heart has been changed, and I am filled with the exquisite joy of the gospel of Jesus Christ," one servant declared.

"It is the same with me," said another. "And I have no more desire to do evil." Each servant spoke earnestly and reverently.

One, a shepherd, came toward Mishgar and knelt as he testified to the gathered crowd. But he seemed to be talking especially to Mishgar as he declared, "I have seen an angel, and he talked to me, just as I am talking to you. He taught me of God and of His righteousness."

Matthew looked on, awed by the Spirit of God, which seemed to fill the chamber. "Do you feel that?" Matthew asked Gid in a low voice.

When Gid did not answer, Matthew turned and discovered his Lamanite friend wrapped in Mishgar's loving arms. As father and son shared their new-found joy in the gospel of Jesus Christ, their embrace grew even stronger. And, as they stood cheek to cheek, tears of gratitude and happiness flowed freely down their faces.

Chapter Nine

The Power of God

The sun hung just over the horizon, casting a golden glow on the city. Rays of fading sunlight filtered across the evening sky, coloring the clouds with warm shades of orange and yellow and pink. Reluctantly, the crowds who were summoned to the palace by Abish's earnest pleadings made their way home before nightfall.

"In all my days, I have never seen and heard such marvelous things as I have today. How I wish Mother had been with us," Mishgar lamented.

"Let us tell her when we get home, shall we, Father?" Gid comforted him.

"Yes, son, we shall," Mishgar smiled, "but first I must check on the animals at the king's stables. With four extra sets of hands, the work will go much faster.

Will you help me?" Mishgar asked the children, with a hopeful look.

"Are there horses?" Peter inquired.

"Yes, lots of horses," Gid replied.

"Then let's go!" Peter replied eagerly.

Katie nudged Matthew, "We ought to leave soon, don't you think?" Matthew nodded, and announced to Gid and Mishgar, "We would love to help, but afterward we will have to start for home. Our family is expecting us."

"We'll hurry then," Mishgar promised. "Come this way." They all walked along the narrow, twisting streets until they came to the outskirts of the city. Mishgar led them to a large, low building with a set of thick wooden doors. He lifted the heavy metal latch, swung wide the doors, and entered.

They were in the king's stables. Rows of stalls lined the enclosure. Each stall held one of the king's horses. Peter could hardly contain his excitement. He had never seen so many strong, beautiful horses, and he wasted no time greeting each one.

A servant was pitching fresh hay into the feeding troughs at the front of each stall.

"Sam," Mishgar called to him, "where are the rest of the men?"

"They are not here. My daughter came to tell us that Abish, the queen's servant, was summoning everyone to the palace. Apparently Abish claimed that God was at work there, and that everyone should go and see the miracles He wrought," Sam explained. "Without a word, the other servants dropped their tools and ran straight to the palace."

"So why are you still here?" Mishgar asked. "Didn't you want to go, too?"

"Yes," Sam said, "but someone had to stay behind to care for the animals."

Humbled by Sam's selflessness, Mishgar quickly picked up a discarded pitchfork and began pitching hay right alongside him.

"You do not need to help here," Sam protested. "After all, you are the chief shepherd. Surely you have more important things to do."

Mishgar stopped, put a hand on each of Sam's shoulders, and spoke to him sincerely. "We serve the same king, Sam. I am pleased to work at your side until the work is done." Mishgar couldn't help remembering Ammon's faithful service to the king.

Mishgar and Sam worked in silence, until Sam had the courage to ask, "Mishgar, did it all happen the way Abish said it did? Were the king and queen really lying on the floor, overcome by the Spirit of God?"

Mishgar leaned on his pitchfork and nodded his head, "Yes, my friend. It happened just as she said it did. Abish knew it was the power of God that had come upon them. She was sure that if the people would come and see, they would believe in the power of God, too."

"It took great courage for her to make known that she had believed in God for many years, and then to persuade the whole city to come and witness God at work," Sam said with admiration in his voice.

"Yes, it did," Mishgar agreed. "Because of her courage, many of the people who went to the royal chamber now believe in God and in his gospel."

"Mishgar, are you one of those people? Do you believe in God?" Sam was beseeching Mishgar with real intent.

Katie, Matthew, and Peter, who had been listening carefully to this conversation, held their breaths.

"Yes, Sam, I do," Mishgar responded, his voice filled with emotion. "Today, when one of the servants of the court awakened, he knelt, looked in my eyes, and testified that he had seen an angel."

"He saw an angel?" Sam could hardly believe it.

"Yes, he did. All of them did—the king, the queen, and all the servants who were overcome. As this servant testified to me, I felt I could see deep into his soul. And I knew he spoke the truth. As I heard his words, I felt God's power flow through every part of my body, until I was completely filled with his Spirit."

As Mishgar testified to Sam, he was again filled

with the Spirit of God, just as before. How he wanted Sam to feel it, too! Mishgar met Sam's sincere gaze, and declared, "It is true, Sam. What the servant said is true. There is a God. And His Son, Jesus Christ, is coming soon to the earth to redeem us all."

As Sam listened to Mishgar's testimony, he felt the power of God's spirit flow into his body, just as Mishgar had described. "I believe your words, Mishgar. No, it is more than that. I know," he said, his voice choked with tears. "I know that what you have told me is true. God lives, and His Son, our Redeemer, shall save us all."

"You feel it, too, Sam. You feel it, too." And Mishgar embraced his fellow believer warmly. "We shall talk more later," Mishgar assured Sam, "but now I must get home to my wife. I want to share with her all I have seen and heard. Good-bye, Sam, until tomorrow. Come, children," Mishgar beckoned to his son, and his son's three friends—two young boys and a girl with her hair swathed in a long, red scarf.

Outside the stable, Matthew asked Gid, "Which way to the clearing where we first met you?"

"Take this road to the corner, turn right into a wide pathway and follow it for a time. You will soon come to the clearing," Gid said, pointing the way. Then he asked, "Will you ever be back, Matthew? I think you and I could be really good friends."

"Maybe we will be back someday, but America is far away." *You have no idea just how far,* Matthew thought to himself.

"Good-bye, then, and God be with you, my new friend," Gid replied, clasping Matthew's hand in a warm handshake.

Mishgar slipped his arm around his son's shoulder, and father and son walked happily together toward their home and their new life—a life filled with the power of God.

The sun slipped behind the hills as the children made their way to the edge of the city and down the shepherds' path to the clearing where they had first arrived.

"I guess it's time to go," Katie said wistfully. She took Gid's sash off of her head and carefully hung it over a branch, where Gid would be sure to find it when he came through with the king's sheep.

She offered one hand to Matthew and the other to Peter. Just before taking hold, the children took a long look around them. To one side of the clearing, sheep grazed safely, no marauding robbers in sight.

To the other side, the city could be seen, the king's palace rising majestically at its center.

This was the palace where Ammon, the missionary, fearlessly preached the gospel in all its glory. And this was the palace where King Lamoni would now rule in righteousness, guided by the matchless power of God.

Chapter Ten

How Great Shall Be Your Joy

As always, when the children returned, Grandma was sitting in her rocking chair reading, as if nothing unusual had happened.

"'And it came to pass that there were many that did believe in their words; and as many as did believe were baptized; and they became a righteous people, and they did establish a church among them . . .'"

"So that's what happened to Gid and Mishgar!" Peter blurted out.

"Who?" Grandma asked.

Matthew elbowed Peter in the ribs. "Why don't we let Grandma finish the chapter, buddy?"

"Oh, fine!" Peter grabbed his side where he had been poked and made a face at his brother.

Thankfully, Katie stepped in. "Hey, Peter, come sit here by me." Peter slid over next to Katie, and the big sister slipped her arm around her younger brother. "Go on, Grandma," she urged, "we're listening."

"'And thus the work of the Lord did commence among the Lamanites; thus the Lord did begin to pour out his Spirit upon them; and we see that his arm is extended to all people who will repent and believe on his name.'"

"Well, that is quite a story, isn't it?" Grandma said, as if she could hardly take it all in. "What did you think of that?"

"I think that is the most exciting one we've seen yet!" Peter replied enthusiastically.

"I think you mean the most exciting one we've *heard,* don't you, Peter?" Katie coached her brother with a knowing wink.

"Right! The most exciting one we've heard," Peter quickly corrected himself.

"What made it so exciting to you?" Grandma asked. "Matthew, you go first."

"Well," Matthew thought for a moment, and then answered, "I suppose it would have to be when Lamoni, the queen, Ammon, and all the servants woke up and started testifying about what they had seen. It was amazing! I never thought about what it would be like to talk to an angel before. But it must have been wonderful, because you could tell that all those people were changed forever."

"Man! I wish I could change for even one day!" Peter said.

Grandma laughed. "I know just how you feel. It is hard to change for good, isn't it? But when you feel—let's see how they say it in the scriptures—yes, here it is, when you feel 'the power of God,' it's easier. At least it is for me."

"I think the power of God is another way to describe the Holy Ghost," Matthew offered thoughtfully. "When I feel the Holy Ghost in my heart, it's easier for me to do the right thing, too, Grandma."

"You have learned some valuable lessons, my boy," Grandma said, touched by Matthew's understanding. She turned to Peter. "How about you, Peter? What did you learn?"

"Well, first off, I learned that Ammon was super-strong, like when he cut off the robbers' arms. But he didn't just have strong muscles. He was strong because God was helping him."

"Very good," Grandma sounded impressed. "Anything else?"

"Well, I learned that when you serve people, they like you better. And you like them better, too."

"Really." Grandma was interested. "How so, Peter?"

"Just think what would have happened if Ammon hadn't served Lamoni. First, Ammon wouldn't have been there to save the king's sheep. Then, Lamoni would never have listened to what Ammon had to say, and he wouldn't have learned about the gospel," Peter said.

Grandma glowed. She loved to hear her grandchildren's insights. She always learned something new—and important—from them.

"All right, Katie, my girl, how about you?"

Katie didn't even have to think. "I learned the most from Abish."

"Yes, that is one of my favorite parts too," Grandma nodded. "What is it you learned, dear?"

"She was faithful, and courageous, and loyal. It made me think about my friend, Aubrey. I want to tell her about the gospel, but I've been afraid to do it because . . ." Her voice trailed off.

"Because what?" Grandma prompted her.

"I didn't want things to change between us. But now I think I can see how to do it." Katie sounded happy and determined.

"Let's hear it, Sis," Matthew encouraged her.

"Okay, last night you said the way you'd go about sharing the gospel is to get to know someone first and then tell them about God," Katie began.

"That's right," Matthew agreed.

"Well, I've done that part. Aubrey is becoming one of my dearest friends," Katie said.

"And you said you thought it would help to serve her, right?" Matthew reminded his sister.

"Right, and I've done that, too. Aubrey knows she can count on me whenever she needs me," she said.

"Now all you need is some courage!" Peter piped up.

"That's just what I was thinking." Katie was glad that Peter had cut right to the chase. "I need courage, just like you, little brother." She ruffled Peter's hair with a smile. "Courage, mixed with faith. That's a good recipe for getting the job done, don't you think?"

"Sounds good to me," Grandma said.

"When I saw how happy Lamoni and the queen and their servants were, I knew I couldn't deny Aubrey the chance to have that happiness too."

"That's just how I felt too." Grandma said closing her eyes, a hint of a smile crossing her lips. The children sat up straight and looked quizzically at each other, wondering what exactly Grandma meant. But Grandma just rocked back and forth in her chair, lost in thought.

Had Grandma been to Lamoni's palace too? None of her grandchildren knew how to ask. They waited patiently until the smile faded from Grandma's face, and her eyes flickered open.

"Oh, yes, darlings! You're here," she said, almost as if she had forgotten their presence. "I was just thinking about how wonderful it must be to hear the gospel for the first time, and to feel the Holy Ghost witness that it's true."

"I never thought of it that way, Grandma. My testimony has grown little by little, because I have been taught all the way along, by my parents, my teachers, and . . . of course, you," Matthew said thoughtfully.

Then Peter remembered the power of the king, the queen, and all the servants testifying together. "Yeah! I think it helps to be taught by lots of believers, sometimes. Hey!" A light went on for Peter. "Why don't we invite Aubrey and her family to family home evening? That way we all could teach the gospel, and Katie won't have to go it alone. Besides,"

now he looked a little impish, "we could all have some fun at the same time!"

"Peter, you always have a way of getting right down to it, don't you? I'll see if they can come this Monday night," Katie said gratefully.

"I thought you were too scared," Matthew teased his sister.

"Not anymore! I can't wait to be the Lord's missionary, just like Ammon and Abish," Katie proclaimed confidently.

"You start writing in your journals, and I'll go get lunch ready," Grandma said, as she tiptoed through her grandchildren, who had sprawled on the art cottage floor, their journals before them.

As Grandma walked down the flagstone path, she thought of her three young missionaries, busily writing in their journals. The song her grandmother taught her came again to her mind, and she sang as she walked:

For if I help but one soul hold fast the iron rod,
How great shall be the joy I feel when I return to God.

"Yes, dear children," Grandma thought, as she smiled from ear to ear. "How great shall be your joy!"

About the Authors

Alice W. Johnson, a published author and composer, is a featured speaker for youth groups, adult firesides, and women's seminars. A former executive in a worldwide strategy consulting company, and then in a leadership training firm, Alice is now a homemaker living in Eagle, Idaho, with her husband and their four young children.

Allison H. Warner gained her early experience living with her family in countries around the world. Returning to the United States as a young woman, she began her vocation as an actress and writer, developing and performing in such productions as *The Farley Family Reunion*. She and her husband reside in Provo, Utah, where they are raising two active boys.

About the Illustrators

Jerry Harston held a degree in graphic design and illustrated more than thirty children's books. He received many honors for his art, and his clients included numerous Fortune 500 corporations. Jerry passed away in December 2009.

Casey Nelson grew up the oldest of eight children in a Navy family, so they moved quite often during her childhood. Graduating with a degree in illustration, she taught figure drawing in the illustration department at Brigham Young University, worked as an artist for video games, and performed in an improvisational comedy troupe. Casey is employed by the Walt Disney Company as a cinematic artist for their video games.